The Blacksmith's Reluctant Bride

Mail Order Brides of Dayton Falls

(Book Four)

Copyright

Copyright ©2019 Cheryl Wright

Dedication

To Margaret Tanner, my very dear friend and fellow author, for her enduring encouragement and friendship.

To Alan, my husband of over forty-eight years, who has been a relentless supporter of my writing and dreams for many years.

To You, my wonderful readers, who encourage me to continue writing these stories. It is such a joy knowing so many of you enjoy reading my stories as much as I love writing them for you.

Table of Contents

Copyright.. 2

Dedication 3

Table of Contents 4

Chapter One.. 6

Chapter Two 13

Chapter Three 19

Chapter Four... 26

Chapter Five 34

Chapter Six... 40

Chapter Seven 50

Chapter Eight.. 55

Chapter Nine 60

Chapter Ten 67

Chapter Eleven 72

Chapter Twelve 77

Chapter Thirteen 84

Chapter Fourteen 91

Chapter Fifteen 99

Chapter Sixteen 105

Epilogue 108

From the Author 110

About the Author 111

Links 112

Chapter One

Westlake, Wyoming – 1880

Amelia Bronson stared down at the two freshly dug graves, tears streaming down her face.

She held tight to the umbrella that sheltered her from the relentless rain, and stared as water seeped into the two coffin-filled graves.

She was wet through, but didn't seem to notice.

Before the tragedy, she was living a happy carefree life.

She sobbed quietly.

At the tender age of twenty, she had lost both her parents in one foul swoop in an accident involving horses and a buggy. She didn't want to know more.

Uncle Cyrus, her father's only other living relative, had moved into the family home since the accident.

She didn't know him well, as he'd always distanced himself from the family, after her father and Cyrus had fallen out before she was born.

No matter, he had inherited everything. She couldn't believe her father had neglected to update his will when she was born, or at the very least, make some kind of provision for her. But that was Papa, always absent minded and too trusting.

"Amelia," Uncle Cyrus shouted from behind her. "It's time to go."

Not that he cared, she was certain of it, but she wanted to spend more time with her parents. All he was interested in was their possessions. And of course, their money.

She sighed. She didn't care about having a lot of money, just enough to live on. Now there wasn't even that, which meant her entire future was at stake.

"Coming, Uncle," she said meekly, for her uncle was known for expecting women to be intimidated by men. Or that should be intimidated by him?

According to Cyrus, women were the weaker of the two sexes; men more dominant and infinitely more important in every way.

She'd heard him express that opinion herself. She shivered inwardly.

Amelia had no idea where she would live, or indeed, *how* she would live. With no income of her own, and no prospects, her future seemed bleak.

* * *

Cyrus Bronson sat back and rubbed his belly. It was full, but he wasn't satisfied.

His stupid niece had never cooked a meal in her life, and what she'd cooked for supper was disgusting. Barely edible.

She'd been spoiled by servants. Her mother was no better.

Why had he let them all go? He wouldn't have had he realized how useless she was.

Amelia stood to clear away the supper dishes, and clean up. He watched her every move.

She might not be good for cooking, but she was ripe for the picking, and he intended to take her as his own.

Tonight.

He would wait until she was asleep and would sneak into her room.

He licked his lips at the prospect.

Amelia turned back and stared at him. "Was supper to your liking, Uncle," she asked innocently, misinterpreting his actions.

He smiled. Not at her words, but at the thought of what he would get later tonight.

"It was," he lied, and she turned back to what she was doing.

Tonight, this fresh young thing would be mine.

* * *

Amelia lay on the bed sobbing, as she had done every night since her parents' demise.

She couldn't stay here with Uncle Cyrus – she feared for her future, but she feared him more than anything else.

He had always been creepy, rubbing himself against her in the most disgusting ways.

Mother had warned her never to find herself alone with him, but would never say why.

She'd shrugged it off when she was younger, but since the accident, she'd begun to understand.

Only now she had no choice. She was living alone with him in her parent's house. The house that should have been hers.

By law it was her uncle's house now, and she couldn't make him leave.

She readied herself for bed and climbed in under the covers, knowing her tear-streaked face would be red and blotchy.

Her eyes fell on the bedroom door, and she quickly jumped out of bed, securing the lock before climbing back in.

She'd made a habit of locking the door since the day Uncle Cyrus had moved into the mansion. She said a silent prayer of thanks for the day her father had insisted a young girl needed her privacy, and had arranged installation of the lock.

She soon fell into a deep sleep, but awoke with a start some time later.

The room was dark, and at first she thought she must have been dreaming.

She lay snuggled into her pillow and covers, and closed her eyes again.

The rattle of the door handle shocked her awake again.

She wasn't mistaken. Someone was trying to get into her room.

No, not someone. Uncle Cyrus!

Mother was right – he was not to be trusted, and this was proof. If she hadn't remembered to lock her door, what might have happened?

Her heart pounded as he continued to try and force the lock.

He now pounded on the door, giving no pretense to his actions, and the entire door rattled, threatening to give in to his persistent hammering.

She heard expletives come from his mouth as the door refused to give way, then silence.

Had he given up?

She breathed a sigh of relief and prepared to sleep again. Until she heard heavy footsteps heading for her room again.

She should have known. Mother always said he was nothing if not relentless.

Amelia had to act fast. She couldn't allow her uncle to force himself on her, as was obviously his intention.

Having no time to dress, she pulled a thick coat over her nightgown, then quickly pulled a few changes of clothes into her carpetbag.

She reached into the drawers next to her bed, looking for any coins she could find. Thankfully, there was quite a stash there.

She threw her bag out first. As she climbed out of her bedroom window and dropped to the ground, she heard the door give way.

At first there was silence, then she heard a tirade of expletives from her uncle.

Her quick thinking had saved her.

Now she had to work out what to do next.

Chapter Two

Amelia wandered around town in the dark trying to find Elizabeth's home.

Mother and Father had always drummed into her about the unsavory characters who wandered around Westlake after dark.

She and Elizabeth had been best friends all through school, and had kept in touch since Elizabeth had married.

With no lantern to find her way, Amelia kept as close to the buildings as possible. It had taken a while, but her eyes had adjusted to the darkness, allowing her to see silhouettes ahead of her.

Her heart pounded as she quickly walked along the silent street. She could see people moving up ahead, and was startled when someone jumped out in front of her.

"Where are you going, my lovely?" a quiet voice asked through the darkness.

Heart pounding, she pushed past him and rushed forward.

A hand snaked out and grabbed her arm. "It's not safe out here for the likes of you." It was a woman's voice this time. "Here, take this lantern. Or better still, I'll take you to your destination."

Amelia stared into her barely-lit face. The woman was much older than herself, perhaps around her mother's age, and seemed street-wise.

"I'll…I'll be alright," Amelia said quietly, before a lantern was shoved in her face.

The woman shook her head. "You won't. I'll take you to wherever you are determined to go at this ungodly hour," she said. "The streets can be dangerous."

She wasn't going to give up, and Amelia had to admit she was frightened. But nowhere near as scared as she had been earlier when Uncle Cyrus had tried to… She wasn't going to think about it.

Too late, she already had, and now tears stung the back of her eyes.

The woman pulled her aside, and sat her on a step in an empty doorway. "I'm Martha," she said. "What's your name?"

Amelia told her, and for some unknown reason felt drawn to the woman sitting next to her. Whether it was because she seemed nurturing, she didn't know. Or it may have been the woman reminded Amelia of her own dear mother; she wasn't sure. But she told Martha the whole story, ending on a river of tears.

"You poor dear," Martha said, holding Amelia's hand and hugging her. "I'll get you safely to your friend's house. It's not safe wandering around alone in the dark."

Amelia wiped her tears on the back of her coat sleeve, and looked the older woman in the eyes. "You'd do that for me?" she asked. "A complete stranger?"

Martha pulled her lips into a tight line. "Wish someone had done it for me when I first hit the streets," she said.

She stood and pulled Amelia up with her, hooking her arm through the younger woman's arm.

"Now tell me your friend's address and we'll be off," she said, holding the lantern out in front.

They walked for what seemed forever, then she suddenly stopped. "This be it," she said, pushing Amelia toward the door.

"I, I can't. Not at this hour." Amelia pleaded with her words and her eyes.

"You can, and you will." She gave Amelia an almighty shove, looking about for any threats to their safety.

The younger woman tapped lightly at first, but yielding no results she knocked harder. She could hear male voices in the distance. Soon she was pounding.

Suddenly the door was wrenched open. A man stood in the doorway wearing nothing but his night gown. For a moment he stared, then shook his head as though trying to clear it.

"Amelia," he exclaimed. "What are you doing here at this hour. How did you get here?" He looked more than a little confused.

"I…" She looked back over her shoulder, but Martha was gone.

"Elizabeth," he called. "It's Amelia."

He showed her into the house, closing the door firmly behind them.

Her friend hugged her tight, and listened as Amelia told her the whole sordid story, including her uncle's unwanted advances.

Her eyes filled with tears again, much to her disgust, and her friend put the kettle on the stove.

"Of course you will stay here with us," she said gently. "I have an idea that will get you away from Westlake and your uncle, and secure your future – all at the same time."

* * *

Samuel Thomas stirred the beans in the pan, at the same time rescuing the toast he'd almost burned on the fire.

It was not the first time this week he'd eaten this meal, if you could call it that, and it surely wouldn't be the last.

He'd asked around – several of the men in Dayton Falls had taken on a mail order bride.

Without any eligible women in town, they'd had little choice.

It was an option he'd strongly resisted, but his resistance was quickly wavering.

He couldn't continue to run his blacksmith's shop and look after himself and his home.

He pulled out the piece of paper he'd shoved into his pocket earlier in the day when he'd visited the Mercantile.

Edward Horvard was happily married to his mail order bride, and they had recently welcomed their first baby.

The barber and the sheriff had both done the same thing. The town was slowly filling up with women and children, which couldn't be a bad thing.

Not that he wanted a bride, no siree. He had no need for a wife in the true sense of the word.

He needed someone who would feed him, clean his house, and wash his clothes. Nothing more, and certainly nothing less.

As he waited for the beans to heat, he pulled down a clean sheet of paper.

Blacksmith needs wife to cook and clean.

He read it back over. That made it sound like he wanted a servant, which he probably did, but he didn't have to force the issue.

He screwed up the paper and started over.

Good Christian man in need of wife. Goes to church each Sunday, and runs a thriving business.

That sounded much better. If he couldn't attract a wife with that advertisement, he never would.

He addressed the envelope and would post it in the morning.

Pete at the post office was the one who started all this. He took on the first mail order bride, and convinced the other men to do the same.

Samuel sniffed, then jumped up as his beans began to burn. "Blasted mail order brides," he snapped, before pouring the burned beans onto his tin plate.

He stared at the envelope. Would he even bother to post it?

Chapter Three

Miss Bethany Wilde of the *Westlake Mail Order Bride Agency* sat opposite the two young women.

"It's highly irregular," she said, looking them up and down. "Although I do admit to having been in this position before."

"I simply cannot wait," Amelia told her. "If my uncle should discover where I am…" She began to cry and her dear friend Elizabeth, who'd insisted on accompanying her today, comforted her.

"Your disgusting uncle will not get near you," Elizabeth said. "Surely you can help out, Miss Wilde?"

The older woman shuffled papers about on her desk. "Everyone calls me Miss Bethany," she said absently, staring at a small bundle of papers in her hand.

"There's a small town in Montana." she said. "I've sent a few young women there, and it's worked out beautifully."

She handed over two pieces of paper. "These are all I have at the moment – in that town at least. If we had more time…"

"But we don't," Elizabeth interjected. "One of these will have to do." She reached out and took the letters, handing them to her friend.

"It's not much, I know. But Dayton Falls is a lovely little town. Some of the other brides have written to tell me so." Miss Bethany leaned back in her seat, and placed her intertwined hands on the desk.

Amelia read over the letters, going between the two. "They're both in business, according to these letters. It makes it very hard to decide."

She turned to Miss Bethany, imploring her to make the choice for her. "I'm sorry, dear, but the decision must be yours."

Amelia muttered under her breath. "Well that's just wonderful," she said quietly.

"Really Amelia, just pick one." When she didn't, Elizabeth folded the letters in four, then put them behind her back, shuffling them around.

"Left or right?"

She hesitated, then made her decision. "Left." Amelia held her breath as her friend opened the letter.

"It's the blacksmith."

Amelia wasn't sure how she felt about that. After all she hadn't been able to decide between him and the shoemaker.

She shrugged. What difference was it anyway?

"That's settled then," Miss Bethany said cheerfully. "You'll need to write a letter and introduce yourself."

Elizabeth stood quickly. "Goodness me, no," she said suddenly. "Amelia must leave immediately. If her uncle discovers her staying with my husband and me, goodness knows what might happen."

"I *must* leave tonight," Amelia said vehemently. She'd never been so forceful in her life, but this was painfully important.

"Of course, of course." Miss Bethany scribbled off a note with the details and handed it over. "I will send a telegram to your young man, and let him know you're coming."

The two women stood to leave. "Keep safe," Miss Bethany told them as she escorted them to the door.

* * *

"Blast," Samuel said as the postmaster handed him the telegram. "I really don't need this today."

"Sorry, Samuel," Pete said. "But I'm compelled by law to deliver it."

Samuel flicked a dirty hand across the front of himself. "I know, and I'm sorry. I didn't meant to take it out on you."

"You mark my word," Pete said. "You'll be happy with your bride. I certainly am. I mean, what isn't there to love? Meals cooked, house cleaned, and all for free. What more could a man ask for?" He waggled his eyebrows, and Samuel laughed out loud.

"I guess there's that about it," he said. "She will be here tomorrow, so I have a bit of time to prepare."

"Samuel," Pete said sharply. "You need to read that telegram again. She'll be here on the next train. Today."

He checked his pocket-watch. "Blast! That's in a few minutes. I'd better get down there."

"I'm sorry, I couldn't get here earlier," Pete told him.

He brushed Pete's apologies aside and stuffed the telegram into his pocket. He quickly locked up the blacksmith's shop, shoving the postmaster out the door.

"But Samuel," Pete protested to deaf ears. Samuel was having none of it.

He almost ran to the train station, still debating with himself if he'd done the right thing organizing a mail order bride.

Too late now, she's almost here.

All he could think was he might have something other than beans for supper. That was at least one positive.

The train pulled in as he arrived at the busy station. The station master was standing on the platform, ensuring all went to plan.

Samuel looked around. *How would he recognize her?*

A young woman stepped out of one of the carriages carrying a large suitcase. Could this be his bride? He took a step forward, until an older man walked up and hugged her.

He stood back. Surely she would look for him? Not that either of them knew what the other looked like. There'd been no time for photographs. Heck, there'd been no time for letters.

"Blast," he said under his breath. This was not the way he'd planned it. He wanted to choose his wife. To get to know her before he agreed to the marriage.

This was not how it was supposed to go!

The blast of the train whistle startled him. Steam filled the platform, and he still hadn't found his bride.

When the steam cleared, there was one young woman left standing on the platform. She was alone and held a small carpetbag. He expected her to bring much more.

Surely this must be his bride. Otherwise she had missed her train.

He stepped toward her, but she turned away and spoke to the station master. He pointed in the direction of Dayton Falls.

Now he was confused. Was this his bride or not? Surely she would stay and wait to be collected if it was her? He pulled the crumpled telegram out of his pocket and double-checked the name.

He ran toward her. "Miss Bronson?" he said, almost breathless. "Miss Amelia Bronson?"

He was bent over trying to regain his breath. He waited for her to speak, instead she stared at him.

No, she thoroughly glared at him.

This wasn't going to end well.

"Please tell me you're not Samuel Thomas," she said quietly, looking him up and down.

By now he'd regained his composure and stood tall. He obviously wasn't what she'd expected.

"I am he," Samuel said proudly. "Samuel Thomas. Your betrothed."

Her face drained of all color. "Mr Samuel Thomas the blacksmith?" she whispered.

"The very one," he said, and thrust his hand forward. It was then he understood the reason for her dismay.

His hands were black from his work, as no doubt his face was. When he looked himself over, he wore his dirty leather apron.

The beautiful young woman who stood before him was more pale than an albino horse, and looked ready to collapse.

"Blast," he said under his breath.

She shuffled about on the spot.

His new bride was about to abscond. Would he be putting her on the next train home?

Chapter Four

Amelia knew the moment the full impact of her situation had hit home.

She felt the color drain from her face, and was suddenly light-headed. Giddy.

You will not faint, she told herself repeatedly.

She couldn't imagine trying to clean the filth out of her gown – one of her best – if the blacksmith caught her going down.

Instead she grabbed hold of the fence leading out into the town of Dayton Falls.

What on earth had she gotten herself into?

The alternative was even less appealing.

She dropped her bag to the ground and stood tall, composing herself.

She took several deep breaths.

Refined women did not faint, Mother had taught her, and she would not disrespect her mother.

"I'm very pleased to meet you, Mr Thomas," she said in a quiet voice. One she didn't recognize as her own.

Young ladies must always behave in an acceptable manner, Mother always said. And that's exactly what she would do.

Even if it meant telling lies, she'd asked. Mother had patted her hand and smiled.

"I'm sorry about my appearance," he said briskly, frowning. "I just got the telegram, you see," he continued. "I shut up shop immediately and ran down here so you wouldn't be standing alone."

She managed a brief smile, but her relief was palpable. Tears threatened at the back of her eyes.

"It's not safe," he added.

For a minute there, she was certain she'd be hightailing it on the next train home.

She stiffened.

But of course she couldn't do that. Her uncle and his disgusting behavior had seen to that.

"Oh," she said, totally relieved. At first she'd thought he was just being disrespectful. "I'm sorry you had to rush," she said, playing with her crumpled skirts.

Underneath all that dirt, he looked nice. Handsome even.

She wondered what he would look like once he'd cleaned up.

He reached down and picked up her bag. Pitiful as it was, it contained all the worldly goods she still possessed.

"This way," he said, pointing ahead of him, careful not to touch her gown. She appreciated the gesture. "It's not far."

She stopped when they reached the township. It took her breath away.

Never in her life had she seen such a quaint little town. Mother and Father had taken her all over the countryside, but never somewhere as beautiful as this.

"It's lovely," she said excitedly. "I'm from Westlake, Wyoming. It's huge compared to this. It's almost a city."

She stared down the main street, and nodded, then turned to him. "I like it," she said quietly.

"Good," he said, and continued.

She chuckled. "You don't say much, do you?"

He stared at her. "No point wasting words that aren't needed."

Oh dear. This could be difficult, because she on the other hand loved to talk. She could sit and chat all day long.

She could see a lot of one-sided conversations in her future.

He suddenly stopped outside a large building and unlocked the enormous door. "This is us," he said, then closed the door again once she was inside. "Up the back."

He really was a man of few words.

She glanced around as they walked through the blacksmith's shop. It was dirty and it was smelly, and there was mess everywhere.

If she hadn't been such a lady, she'd probably be gagging by now.

"Can you cook," he asked as he unlocked the door to the residence. "I'm right sick of beans."

She stared at him then couldn't help herself. A giggle bubbled up and there was no way she could stop it.

He glared at her as she stood there giggling, probably wondering what the heck he'd got himself into.

"What's so funny," he snapped, then walked inside, depositing her carpetbag on the bed.

It was his room, she was certain. There was a large bed in the middle of the room, with a window to one side.

Near the window was a kitchen chair, and it had men's clothes strewn over it. The wardrobe door stood open, and there hung more men's clothes.

Her breath caught in her throat. Did he expect her to sleep with him straight away? They were complete strangers. He didn't know her, and she certainly didn't know him.

"I, I can't sleep here," she said quietly, her voice shaking.

"We'll be married within the hour," he snapped. "There ain't no other bed."

He glared at her again and stormed out of the room. "I'm gonna clean up and we'll get married then," he said over his shoulder.

Amelia collapsed on the side of the bed. What had she gotten herself into? This man, this Samuel Thomas, he didn't want a wife.

No, he wanted someone to cook for him. Perhaps what he really wanted was a maid.

She let the full impact of that wash over her.

She looked up when she heard him shuffling in the doorway. "I put clean water for you," he said. "And a fresh towel. Get cleaned up and we'll find the preacher."

"I, I'm not sure I want to…"

"Blast it, woman," he snapped. "You came here willingly. I'm not gonna force you."

She opened her mouth to speak, but the words wouldn't form.

Amelia stood, then nodded. Without another word she went into the nearby bathroom to clean up. She pulled her long hair down, brushing it using only her fingers, then returned it to its original state.

She used the rough face cloth to clean the remnants of the dirty steam from her face, then washed her arms and hands.

Staring at herself in the mirror, she wasn't certain what to do.

She took some calming breaths. What other option did she have?

She shoved her hand in her skirt pocket and pulled out the few remaining coins.

There really was no choice. She either married Samuel Thomas today, or…

There was no "or". She had too few coins to go anywhere, and she certainly couldn't return to Westlake.

She looked down at her gown. It was grubby but not dirty. She only had one other gown with her. It was at least clean.

"I have to change my gown," she said suddenly, imploring him to leave the bedroom. When he stood rigid, she glared. "Some privacy would be nice," she snapped. "We're not married yet."

A cold chill came over her. She'd just admitted to her future husband he would be able to watch her undress once they married.

He nodded then left the room, closing the door behind him.

"Darn it." She couldn't reach to secure all the fastenings. She had a personal maid to do that.

At least she used to have one. Now she had nothing. All her beautiful gowns were left behind, and all her prized belongings.

Possessions like the stuffed bear Mother had given her on her fifth birthday. And the diamond necklace her parents had surprised her with at her sixteenth birthday party.

Her hands went to her neck. There had been no time to gather up those things that meant the most to her.

She fought back a sob, then opened the door. "Mr Thomas," she said abruptly. "Can you please fasten my dress?"

"Uh…" He stood momentarily frozen. "Of course," he said. "After all, we're about to be husband and wife."

His hands hovered momentarily, then he secured the fastenings, and turned her to face him. "You look very pretty," he said, looking her up and down.

Until that moment she hadn't taken the time to look him over. Now that his face was clean, she could see he was handsome. Very handsome indeed.

"Thank you," she said, fighting the urge to brush back the clump of jet black hair that had fallen across his face.

"We need to go," he said. "I have to get back to work."

She nodded and they left to find the preacher.

Amelia's wedding was nothing like the one she had envisioned.

This one was empty, hollow even. Standing next to a complete stranger saying her forever vows didn't seem right.

The preacher near glared at her. Samuel had warned her he loathed mail order bride weddings, and it showed.

Apart from two townspeople pulled off the street as witnesses, no one was there to see them exchange their vows. Especially not her parents.

She fought back a sob.

Two months ago, her wedding aspirations looked totally different.

A pristine bride in a flowing custom-made white dress, at least one bridesmaid taking up the rear, and a bouquet of fresh and fragrant flowers in her hands.

Best of all, her father with his arm hooked through hers, ready to give her away.

All her family and friends would be in the congregation, waiting in anticipation.

She sighed.

Not even a single rose in sight.

"I have to get back to work," he whispered as they left the church.

Was this really her wedding day? Tears pooled in her eyes, and she turned away to stop her new husband seeing them.

He hooked his arm through hers and headed back to the blacksmith's shop. "When we get back, you might work out what you're doing for supper, then go to the Mercantile and get supplies. Tell Edward to put it on my account."

She startled. *Didn't he realize she couldn't cook?*

She guessed he didn't. How could she tell him?

"You can make anything you like as long as it's not beans." He grinned.

She panicked but said nothing and just nodded.

Amelia followed him into the residence, where he changed from his Sunday best into the dirty blacksmith's clothes he'd worn earlier.

They were abhorrent. How did he work in such filth?

She pottered around in the kitchen for a few minutes and discovered the only items in the pantry were beans and bread.

As she studied the bread, she saw tiny bits of green sprouting out on the crusts. Ugh!

Determined to cook something decent for her husband's supper, with no idea how she would do that, Amelia went looking for the Mercantile.

As the bell tinkled over the door, all eyes turned her way. She prayed for the ground to open up and swallow her.

A tall man in an apron approached her. "Good morning," he said jovially. "I'm Edward Horvard, owner of the Mercantile. And this," he indicated a red-haired beauty. "Is my wife Phoebe."

Amelia felt like she was on display. Everyone continued to stare.

Apparently sensing her discomfort, Mrs Horvard approached her. "Please come in. We're all friends here."

"I," Her mouth was dry. She felt completely out of her depth. "I'm Amelia Bronson." She slapped her hands to her mouth. "Oh! I'm Amelia Thomas. Mr Thomas and I married a short time ago." She felt the heat creep up her neck and face, and she felt ill.

Phoebe reached over and held her hand. "A new bride. How wonderful!" Phoebe exclaimed, as though it was the most wonderful thing in the world.

And she supposed it could be, if being married was what you wanted. If marrying a complete stranger was your life's wish. But if all you wanted to do was save yourself from your repulsive uncle, then that was another thing entirely.

"Are you a mail order bride," Phoebe whispered, ensuring no one else could hear.

Amelia nodded.

"Me too. Give it time, you'll settle in soon enough." She reached over and hugged the new bride. "Now, what can I get you?"

Amelia felt more relaxed knowing she wasn't alone.

"Something for supper. Anything but beans, he said."

Phoebe laughed. "Can you cook," she whispered. It was as though she totally understood Amelia's predicament.

"I, I can't. I don't know what I'm going to do." Tears pooled in her eyes. This seemed to be becoming the norm lately. She was not a crier, and it irritated her that she'd become one.

It was entirely her uncle's fault, and it made her angry.

She was guided to a shelf in the middle of the room. "This book," Phoebe said, picking up a cookbook. "Saved my life." She grinned. "At least it saved my sanity, and my marriage. I promise, it will help you."

"Cookery for the Modern Woman." She flicked through the pages. "I don't know, Thomas didn't say I could get it," she protested, not sure what to do.

Phoebe rubbed her hand across the other woman's back. "I promise you, he'll be happy. But if he's not, bring it back."

Amelia stared at her, then nodded. She couldn't ask for more than that.

"Let's get you some basics, because I'm certain Samuel will have nothing in the pantry." She reached for a box.

"Moldy bread and beans. That's all." She managed a smile this time.

"Right. So eggs, flour, potatoes, butter, and bread. Oh, and milk. You can always come back for more supplies."

"When you get home," Phoebe told her, "Check the pancake recipe. It's very easy, filling, and you have all the ingredients here."

Amelia opened the page to pancakes. It looked simple, but when you've never cooked before…

Phoebe leaned in close. "When you eat beans almost daily, pancakes are a delicacy."

She was probably right. But would it be enough?

"We're open for another few hours. Come back if you need anything else."

Amelia felt incredibly out of her depth. What if she burned the pancakes? What if it was just a lumpy mess?

She straightened her back and left the store. She would give Samuel a meal fit for a king.

At least she hoped she would.

Chapter Six

Amelia sat at the kitchen table flicking through the new cookbook.

She decided on a hearty vegetable soup for supper, and instead of pancakes, she would make biscuits.

They looked to be less complicated than pancakes. Perhaps when she felt more confident she would tackle them.

She spotted paper and a pencil on a shelf, and began to write a list of ingredients she would need.

She would go back to the Mercantile and get enough ingredients to make a stew tomorrow as well.

This time she wouldn't feel like a wilting flower when she walked in. She would stand tall and not act like the newest citizen to Dayton Falls.

She straightened her back, fluffed up her skirts, and walked out the door of the residence.

"Amelia," Samuel called. "Where are you off to?"

She looked back at him over her shoulder. "I'm going back to the Mercantile to get more supplies. I have something special planned for supper."

Despite the dirt that covered his face, his smile transformed him.

"What are you cooking?"

She decided to be bold, and laughed. "It's a surprise. You'll see later."

"Get whatever you need," he called after her. "Anything."

Those few words, uttered as an afterthought helped her relax. He wasn't worried about her buying a cookbook; he was more worried about what went into his belly.

With a swing in her step, she made her way back to the store and chose her extra ingredients, as well as an apron.

She would go home and spring into action.

Home… It wasn't the home she'd lived in for most of her life, and it wasn't where she wanted to be. But it was now her home and she needed to get used to it.

She shook herself. These depressing thoughts would bring her down.

As she walked past him, Samuel took the box from her and carried it into the kitchen.

"There you are, darlin'," he said as they entered, then left.

After he'd gone, Amelia noticed the state of the kitchen.

The table needed a good scrub along with the benches. She opened the oven. It wasn't quite so bad – it probably didn't get much use.

Opening the cupboards she found some soap and brushes to clean the place up.

But first she needed to put on the soup. According to the cookbook, it took some hours.

She scrubbed the chopping board before she dared put food on it, then diced the vegetables as instructed.

Then she began work on sanitizing the kitchen. Even the pantry needed cleaning.

She sighed. This was not the life she had envisioned, but it was the life she'd been forced into. She would make the most of it.

As she scrubbed her way around the room, she realized this kitchen was ill-equipped. In fact it was almost bare.

It comprised of a wood stove, a pantry cupboard, and two big storage boxes under the window.

Apart from that, there was a small table and another cupboard with an enamel bowl where she would wash the soiled dishes. In the corner was a small ice chest, where she'd placed the milk and butter.

It was a far cry from the well-equipped kitchen cook had to work with in her family home.

She sniffed the air. Something was burning. Her soup!

She grabbed the saucepan handle and lifted it from the wood stove. Scraping the only wooden spoon in the drawer, she stirred it gently.

It had just begun to stick, and wasn't truly burned. Thank goodness for small miracles.

She forced herself to stay strong. *It's only soup! Stay focused.*

She returned to the cookbook. What did it say to do in this situation? She scanned the pages carefully.

Add more water and stir gently.

She felt relieved when the food came away from the base of the saucepan when the additional water was added.

Then she went back to scrubbing the table. She couldn't believe the disgusting mess Samuel had left in his kitchen.

She stopped and thought for a moment. It was her kitchen now. And she would never allow it to get this grimy again.

She looked down at her aching hands. They were red raw from all the scrubbing and washing. But it would be worth it in the end.

Would her husband even notice the difference? She thought not. Someone who worked in all that filth day after day, wouldn't notice a dirty kitchen.

That was obviously true because look at the state of it now.

She finished the table and it was like new, it was so clean.

She would scrub out the pantry next, then add the left over supplies she'd bought.

Amelia would need to thoroughly check out the kitchen. No doubt there was little for her to work with, especially when it came to equipment.

She'd need to talk with Samuel, and ensure he was happy for her to purchase the additional equipment needed to provide him with a variety of meals. She couldn't do that with what was available right now.

She put the kettle on the wood stove and prepared to make her husband a cup of coffee. But she had no idea how he liked it.

Her head hurt – there was too much she had to learn. Did Phoebe feel this way when she first arrived?

Amelia decided she must have. The woman had already admitted she was unable to cook then.

She felt a little better knowing she was not as stupid as she appeared.

She stirred the soup again, not willing to let it stick again, then poured her husband a coffee. She made it black, like her father had it, and headed out to the blacksmith's shop.

Like earlier, the pungent odor made her gag. She supposed she'd eventually get used to it, but right now it was appalling to her delicate senses.

The heat was also overwhelming, and she wondered what he did that made it so hot.

As she got closer, the hammering permeated her ears. The noise was tremendous.

"Samuel," she said meekly, not certain she was allowed to call him by his first name.

He totally ignored her. With the level of noise, she wasn't certain he'd even heard her.

She stepped a little closer and touched his shoulder. He startled.

He turned his head to stare at her. "Amelia," he said blandly. Was he unhappy to see her?

"I brought you some coffee." She reached out to hand it to him.

"Just put it over there," he said abruptly. "I don't really have time to drink it."

She swallowed back a sob. Her new husband hated her. She did something nice for him, and he didn't even appreciate it.

She placed the coffee on a nearby bench, then turned and ran back into the residence.

"Amelia," she heard him call after her, but she wasn't hanging around for him to tell her off again.

Besides, she had to check on the soup, and begin work on the biscuits.

Sitting at the kitchen table, Amelia stared down into her cup of tea.

Less than a day as a married woman and her husband was already disappointed in her.

She knew it wasn't going to be easy, but she didn't expect to be treated this way. Like nothing she did was right.

She'd tried to be a good wife, but she had no role model to emulate. Her mother had not cooked in all the years Amelia could remember.

Her father had always been very well-to-do, and they'd had a cook and several servants most of her life.

Cook hated her being in the kitchen, so she never learned the art of preparing food, and it was totally forbidden that she clean anything. She wasn't even permitted to clean her own bedroom.

She lifted the cup to her mouth and took a sip. A slow tear trickled down her face. She brushed it away with her fingers.

"Amelia." His voice was soft. Gentle.

Her head shot up.

He stood tall in the doorway. "Thank you," he said quietly. He lifted the mug to his mouth with grubby hands. "I do appreciate it," he said. "I didn't mean to sound so rude."

He sounded so sincere, and she burst into tears and sobbed. Had she read him completely wrong?

"Good grief woman," he said roughly. "Don't bawl. I can't deal with that."

She wiped at her face and took another sip of tea. "I'm completely fine," she said sternly, then stood and stirred the soup again, effectively dismissing him from her kitchen.

But he stayed planted to the spot, then sniffed. "That smells mighty good." He followed her over to the stove and looked over her shoulder. "It's years since I had home made soup."

"I hope I do it justice," she said softly, enjoying the heat radiating from him.

"I can't wait," he said, rubbing his hands together. "I have to get back to work," he said, then turned to walk away.

He looked back over his shoulder as he reached the doorway. "I'm sorry," he said. "I'm not used to having a woman around. I'll try to do better next time."

She nodded.

"The coffee was good. A man could get used to that."

And then he was gone.

Amelia sighed. Could this work after all? He seemed genuine in his apology. And he certainly appreciated that she'd made soup. She only hoped it tasted good.

She drained the cup then began work on the biscuits. It was still early, but if she messed them up, she would need time to make another batch.

Tonight's supper would be her first. She didn't want it to be her worst.

Chapter Seven

While the biscuits cooked in the wood oven, Amelia began heating water in every container she could find.

Samuel would need a bath before he sat at the table for supper.

The bathroom here was much smaller than what she was used to, but at least there was a decent sized bath, and a water closet.

Some families still endured an outside water closet. She shivered – she was so glad that wasn't an option.

She'd been surprised at finding a porcelain bath. She thought it would be a tin one. Thankfully it wasn't.

She'd turned on the faucets and allowed the cold water to run into the bath. She didn't want Samuel stepping in and burning himself.

She poured in the first round of boiling water, then refilled the containers.

The biscuits must be just about ready now. She grabbed a kitchen towel and opened the oven door.

They were nicely browned and had risen.

She took a deep breath. She hoped they were good inside.

Only one way to find out.

She lifted the hot tray from the oven and placed it on the wooden board, then broke open one of the biscuits.

Her heart raced. Would they be edible, or would she need to start over?

To her surprise, they looked wonderful.

He stood in the doorway and stared, then kicked off his work boots. "What do you have there? It smells good."

"It was supposed to be a surprise," she said softly.

He stared at her momentarily. Did he know it would break her heart if all her surprises were revealed?

"I won't look, I promise," he said, then headed toward the bathroom to clean up.

"Samuel," she shouted after him. "I have more water ready for you."

She snatched up a clean kitchen towel and covered the biscuits, then carried the water to the bath.

He stared at her. "You did this for me?" The emotion in his voice got to her. "I usually just wash up."

"Of course," she said, her voice breaking. "You're my husband." She poured the water into the bath, then checked the temperature.

She reached into the cupboard and pulled out a clean bath towel and face towel for him.

As she began to leave, he pulled his shirt up over his head, and she stared.

She'd never seen a man in any state of undress before. Her heart raced, and she stood mesmerized.

When she looked back at his face he was grinning. Did he think it funny?

She huffed, then scurried away to set the table for supper, pulling the door closed behind her.

"You could scrub my back," he shouted through the door.

"Never," she said quietly.

* * *

"You've done an amazing job," he said, filling his mouth with more soup. "I've had beans for so long, I'd even forgotten other food existed."

It was true. He appreciated every effort she'd made for him today.

The coffee was such a surprise, and he'd annoyed himself at the way he'd barked at her.

Poor Amelia. She must be feeling so confused. He didn't know what happened that she'd had to rush here, but it was obvious she'd been desperate.

It would take both of them some time to get used to the new situation.

She was such a pretty thing, but sadness seem to overwhelm her.

Even when she smiled, there was a great sadness surrounding her. He hoped it would eventually disappear.

"I hope you don't mind," she said softly, not looking at him. "But I bought a cookbook today."

She continued to study the table.

"Amelia," he said, reaching across and touching her chin, turning her face toward him. "I don't mind, I promise. This meal is amazing. The best I've had for as long as I can remember."

He watched as her face transformed from that ever-present sadness into joy.

She wriggled in her seat. "Really?" Her smile lit up her entire face, and he wished she would smile more.

He would make it his mission to make her happy.

He stopped in his tracks. Didn't he decide to a marriage in name only? No love or emotion involved.

Then that's what he would do.

He thought for a moment. He could still make her happy without involving love. Couldn't he?

Besides, they didn't even know each other. How did you love someone you'd never met before?

He snatched up another biscuit and smothered it with butter. "These are really good," he said between bites.

She grinned. "Thank you. I wanted to please you on our first night together."

He felt warm all over, then shook himself mentally. That wasn't part of the deal.

The arrangement was she would cook for him, do the laundry and look after the house. He would effectively give her room and board in exchange.

And that was the deal they would stick to. None of this lovey-dovey stuff. That's not what he signed up for.

His decision made, he sat straighter against the chair and shoveled more food into his mouth.

Chapter Eight

Amelia tidied up the kitchen, and wiped down the table.

Samuel sat in an easy chair in the sitting room. She put her head around the door and saw he was snoozing.

She felt sorry for him – he worked really hard.

It must have been difficult for him before she arrived. Working all day, then having to prepare supper for himself.

No wonder he ate beans all the time. Poor man.

She'd felt completely overwhelmed when she'd arrived, but he'd put her at rest.

Succeeding at supper had helped too.

Samuel seemed to appreciate the efforts she'd gone to for him, and he certainly enjoyed the bath. He'd told her so.

Tomorrow she would have to clean the scum from the bath – make it white again.

But she didn't mind. She was safe here. Uncle Cyrus would never find her, and that was the most important thing to her.

But if he did? Would Samuel protect her, or would he send her away? Perhaps she wasn't worth the trouble.

She looked about. She was happy with the state of the kitchen, and vowed to never let it get in such terrible condition again.

When she stopped, she felt suddenly tired. No, not tired, but exhausted. Physically and emotionally.

The trip had tired her out, but since the wedding ceremony, she'd not stopped all day. She felt like she could drop right where she stood.

With no other option, she would have to retire to Samuel's bed.

She quietly opened the bedroom door, not wanting to disturb his sleep in the other room.

She closed the door gently behind her, then began to undress. She'd had so little to bring with her, but did at least have a nightgown.

She managed to undo the fastenings, and pulled her gown up over her head, laying it on the bed. Next she removed her petticoats, and lay them down as well.

She stood in her drawers and camisole, and was about to remove them when the door quietly opened.

She gasped, and snatched up her petticoats, holding them in front of her.

"You can't be in here," she said urgently.

He stood there grinning at her, scanning her from head to toe. "It's my bedroom," he said. "I can come in. Besides, you're my wife. I'm allowed to look," he said, winking at her.

Oh my.

"I, I…" What did she say to that? What should she do?

She stood there shaking, and staring at him. She had no idea how to respond, and wasn't sure if she should run.

He stepped toward her, and ran his hands down her arms.

It felt nice, and a tingle went through her. She should shake his hands off, but she was frozen to the spot.

His arms went up and around her body, and he held her in a hug, then he breathed in deep.

"You smell nice," he said. She nodded, but words wouldn't form on her lips.

Suddenly he stepped back, and gazed into her face. "I'll let you get undressed. I'll be back shortly." Then he left the room.

She suddenly felt bereft. But she also felt relieved. She hadn't been prepared to be a real wife.

What he'd wanted was something akin to a servant, not a proper wife. Not someone he could hold and love.

Just a housemaid.

She stared at the closed door for about a minute before returning to what she'd been doing before.

Once in her nightgown, she hung her gown up in the wardrobe. There was plenty of room – Samuel didn't have many clothes.

His Sunday best was there, and a pair of tidy slacks and a button up shirt, and that was it.

Did that mean he didn't go out except to church?

Amelia figured she'd eventually find out.

She climbed into bed and snuggled in. It wasn't long before she was sound asleep.

She woke up sometime during the night when two arms wrapped around her and held her tight.

It was nice; it felt good. But she wouldn't let herself get used to it.

This was a marriage of convenience, and nothing more.

59

Chapter Nine

As they strode toward the church, Amelia felt a little overwhelmed.

She didn't know anyone here.

Samuel squeezed her hand. She didn't think anyone could ever understand her so completely, but he did.

The preacher stood at the door greeting the parishioners as they entered. "Good morning Mrs Thomas," he said cheerfully, in total contrast to the way he'd treated her on their wedding day.

"Good morning, Preacher," she answered. Her husband squeezed her hand, then led her to a pew at the back of the little church where they'd married almost a week earlier.

A parishioner had relieved her of the biscuits she'd made for luncheon, as they entered.

As she sat, the organist began to play her most favorite song – Onward Christian Soldiers.

It was also her mother's favorite, and it brought a lump to her throat.

"Good morning, Mrs Thomas," said an older woman sitting next to her. "I'm Bertha Grogan, the doctor's wife."

It helped take her mind off the people she'd lost.

So far, everyone in this tiny town of Dayton Falls had been everything she'd hoped.

Amelia reached for the bible sitting at the back of the pew, holding it for solace.

As if she understood completely, Mrs Grogan reached over and patted her hand. It was comforting.

Her uncle had refused to allow Amelia to attend church after her parents had died, except for their funeral. And that was only because of appearances. What would people say if he didn't allow her to attend her own parents funeral?

Knowing what she knew now, was it any wonder he didn't attend church? The devil himself wouldn't dare to step inside such a sacred place.

It wasn't long before they stood for the first of several hymns, and Amelia was beginning to feel at ease.

When the service was over, several women from the auxiliary greeted her, taking her in hand.

"I'm Allie, this is Charlotte, Mrs Jensen, Mrs Green, and Mrs Jackson," she was told. "You've already met Mrs Grogan."

She was hugged by several of the women, especially the younger ones, and taken to the large kitchen.

"I'm never going to remember everyone's names," she said, but was told not to worry.

The church she'd attended in Westlake was nothing like this. It had a large attendance base, but was not as friendly as this small church.

She smiled at her husband as she spotted him across the room, talking to the Mercantile owner.

She could certainly get used to this lovely little town and it's friendly people.

* * *

Amelia awoke wrapped up in Samuel's arms. She was getting used to waking this way every day, and wasn't complaining.

It felt good to be wanted, and his warmth seeped through to her.

The bed was pretty good too.

He stirred. "Good morning, wife," he said, grinning at her, then rolled away.

She felt empty, and didn't like the feeling at all. "Good morning."

She tried to roll out of bed, but he snaked a hand around her. "I like it better when I'm holding you," he said. "But I have to get ready for work."

She liked it too, it felt nice. She had work to do too, starting with making Samuel's breakfast.

She was getting used to the new routine, and even enjoyed it some days.

She pulled away, then sat on the side of the bed. "It's quiet here," she said, then yawned. "I used to live in a big city – it was always noisy."

She sighed. As much as she hated the noise, she'd had her parents.

She also got to see her friend Elizabeth. That probably wouldn't happen ever again. The very thought made her sad.

She needed to take her mind off such unhappy thoughts. "What would you like for breakfast today?"

She turned to look at her husband. He was in the process of pulling up his drawers.

She gasped.

He turned around and grinned at her. He obviously thought it was funny, but to her, it wasn't.

It was…indecent.

She stared at his bare chest. "You need to put a shirt on, Samuel," she said tersely. "That is not appropriate. Or decent."

He laughed. She liked the sound of him laughing. He didn't do it often enough.

"It would only be indecent if we weren't married," he said. Then his mood changed. He frowned at her and his face was serious. "But we are," he added softly.

"Fine," she told him, then reached for her robe and left the room in a huff.

She could still hear him laughing from the kitchen.

* * *

She added more wood to the stove and stirred it up. It was chilly in there, and she needed to fix it. She would spent most of her day there, so that simply wouldn't do.

She had checked her new cookbook and decided to make her husband scrambled eggs. He seemed to like them.

The kettle was already heating up, and she'd pulled out some bread, ready to make toast.

She set the table while she waited for him to appear. She supposed she'd get used to his cheeky sense of humor, but right now she found it downright irritating.

He entered the kitchen and walked straight toward her, hands outstretched as though he was about to hug her.

"Sit," she ordered, before he starting playing his silly games.

He looked deflated, but it was necessary for her sanity.

Okay, it was for both of them. Neither wanted a real marriage, and the games he played would push them in that direction.

She stirred the eggs, then turned to him. He looked deflated.

As she turned back to the stove, the toast began to burn. "Nooooo!"

She sobbed. She couldn't do anything right. She pulled it off the stove and threw it onto the plate, then stirred the eggs before they burned too.

Samuel stood and made his way toward the burned toast. "It's not that bad," he said, looking it over.

She stared over his shoulder. Perhaps not.

He stood there buttering the toast, while she finished the eggs, then spooned them onto his plate.

"Sit and eat while it's hot. I'll pour the coffee."

He did as he was told. "This is lovely, Amelia," he said between mouthfuls. "Until you arrived, I hadn't had breakfast for a very long time."

"Really?" She continued to be amazed by the things he revealed to her.

"Really."

She stared at his face. He was a very handsome man. When he wasn't covered in dirt, he was good to look at.

Oh, who was she fooling? She reveled in gazing at him. It made her feel good all over.

"Having a good look?" He laughed.

She felt the heat creep up her neck and face.

"Guilty," she said, then laughed too. "You look so different without dirt on your face."

He frowned. "It's not dirt, it's soot," he said. "I'm sorry, but I can't help it. This is what pays the bills."

He shoveled in the last mouthful of his breakfast, then left the table without another word.

She'd insulted him. She truly didn't mean to do that. "Samuel," she called after him, but he ignored her.

Perhaps one day she'd learn to keep her big mouth shut.

Chapter Ten

He was beginning to get used to having Amelia around, and then she says something like that.

It was like a punch to the gut.

He couldn't help that he was grubby by the end of the day. Being a blacksmith was hard work. Hard and dirty work, but he loved it.

He'd been privileged to learn the trade, and then inherit the business from his father who'd died unexpectedly five years ago.

Samuel hadn't anticipated running his own business before he was thirty, but it happened that way.

It had been difficult though.

His mother had always been there for his father, and for him, until she'd died of a heart attack. They'd been standing together talking when she'd clutched her chest and dropped to the ground.

There was nothing anyone could do – she was gone instantly.

Father had been heartbroken, and only lasted another year or so. Rumor was he'd taken his own life, but Samuel knew better. His father was stronger than that.

He'd died of a broken heart.

He had to shake those depressing thoughts away, and worry about the dilemma he was now facing.

Amelia. His pretend wife.

Could they ever have the sort of marriage his parents enjoyed? Did he even want that?

Theirs was a marriage of convenience too, but they seemed happy enough. He wouldn't say blissfully happy, but they certainly weren't unhappy with their lot.

He grabbed a piece of steel and shoved it in the burning embers. Snatching up the hammer, he waiting patiently until the steel was hot enough to manipulate.

He stared across at the residence. What was Amelia doing now? Had he upset her with the way he'd stormed out?

He hoped so.

He bit his bottom lip. He didn't mean that. He liked Amelia – he would never hurt her intentionally.

Samuel wanted to toss the hammer aside and run to her. Tell her he'd been a fool, and apologize for his appalling behavior.

But the piece of steel was ready, and he didn't want to waste it. So instead he took his frustrations out on the heated metal sitting in front of him.

She'd continued to be on his conscious for most of the morning. The only way it would settle would be to go and talk to her.

He decided he had too much to do.

Deep down he knew that wasn't true. All he had to do was put down his tools and go into the residence, apologize, and go back to work.

Oh for goodness sakes!

A week ago he hadn't had to worry about any of this nonsense. It was him, and him alone. Why should he worry about niceties just because he now had a wife.

"Samuel?" He startled at the sound of Amelia's voice. "I've brought you coffee."

She sat it on the table, then lingered. When he didn't respond she turned to leave.

Then it hit him she was waiting for him to say something. "Amelia," he said, feeling guilty for not saying anything before. "Thank you."

She turned back to him and smiled briefly, then turned away again. Evidently she was still upset.

"Please don't leave," he said, then reached out to touch her shoulder. He risked soiling her gown, so yanked off his thick gloves. Samuel needed to talk to her before it ate away at him.

"I'm truly sorry for my behavior at breakfast," he said gently, standing close to her.

"I doesn't matter," she said flippantly. But he knew that wasn't true. He could see it in her eyes, and in the hard set of her face. She was visibly upset, and it was all his fault.

"It does matter," he said genuinely. He reached over and took both her hands in his. "It matters to me, and I can tell it matters to you."

He was enjoying holding her hands. They were soft and gentle, and a warmth flowed through him as he stood there caressing them.

"I, I have to go and organize supper," she said, and tried to pull her hands out of his grip.

He was reluctant to let her go, and put his lips to her hand. His lips tingled.

She wrenched her hand out of his grip, and he felt hollow. He wished they could spend the day together and get to know each other better.

It was an impossible dream as he had many orders to fulfill.

"Thank you again," he said, wondering if that gentle kiss had affected her as much as it had him.

She nodded and walked away.

It was early days yet, but Samuel hoped they could be friends.

Chapter Eleven

As she went about her work, Amelia realized how easy she'd had it her entire life.

The servants did everything, and all she had to do was sit around and look pretty.

That's what her parents had told her repeatedly.

They'd introduced her to several young gentlemen with the sole purpose of marrying her off to a rich family.

But none were rich enough for her father. What would he think of Samuel? Doing hard labor for a living is not what he would approve of.

She stiffened. "I'm sorry Father, Mother," she said quietly, her eyes filling with tears.

Swiping at her eyes, Amelia dragged the laundry into a bucket, ready to hang on the clothes line.

Not that she blamed Samuel, he was a man after all, but the place was in a bad way. When she'd arrived, the bed linen needed washing, and was in such a state, she'd given it first priority.

She promised herself to get the place looking spotless. No one would have the opportunity to judge her as a bad housekeeper. Or a bad wife.

She'd been there such a short time, but already she'd seen her husband's stubborn side.

Amelia wondered if he would ever soften to her. Or would he always keep her at a distance?

Not that she wanted to be his *true* wife, but she did want to at least become friends. This unease she was feeling didn't sit well with her.

After hanging the sheets, she proceeded to cut the vegetables for supper. She was determined to dish up a different meal for supper every night, and tonight she was making a beef stew.

He worked hard, and he deserved to come home to a nice hot meal, and not the beans he'd survived on for so long.

The cookbook she'd bought was proving to be invaluable. She must thank Phoebe next time she saw her.

She was startled when Samuel rushed through the door.

"What are you doing here?" she asked in a panic, wondering why he'd suddenly materialized.

He stared at her momentarily. "It's time for luncheon," he said gently, as though he understood her current state of mind.

"Oh." She been so wrapped up in her work, she hadn't noticed the time. Luckily there were leftover biscuits from last night's supper. And she had extra soup. She would put that on to warm up. "I'm sorry. I've been so busy, I didn't think about it."

He frowned, and she worried he was going to yell at her, the way he had when she first arrived.

"Don't do too much," he said softly. "You need to rest up. You've had a big few days."

He wasn't cross at all. In fact, he was worried about her.

How sweet.

But she couldn't afford to get soft on him. "Sit." She set the soup in the saucepan, then placed a plate of biscuits in front of him, and the kettle on the stove.

"What's for supper?" he asked, reaching for one of the biscuits.

She was reluctant to tell him in case she messed it up. But he'd asked. "If it works out alright, we'll be having beef stew."

He gazed at her for a moment. "You won't mess it up, believe me. You've done so wonderfully with all the meals you've made."

Was he just saying that, or was it really true?

She supposed the soup did turn out fine, so she couldn't really deny that. And the biscuits tasted superb, if she did say so herself.

What they'd be like today was another issue altogether.

She hadn't been very adventurous with the meals so far, but she had served up something different each night.

The soup began to simmer on the stove and she dished up a large bowl for Samuel, and a much smaller one for herself.

He leaned down into and sniffed. "It smells just as good as it did last night." He scooped up a spoon and began to eat. "This really is good," he said, then didn't speak again until it was all gone.

"I'll do better next time." She stood to make his coffee.

He stopped midway of putting a biscuit in his mouth. "You did good this time. A man can't complain about the food you've dished up so far."

The coffee splashed on the table as she set it down. Grabbing up a kitchen cloth, she began to clean it up.

He covered her hand with his own. "Amelia," he said softly.

The zing that ran up her arm frightened her, and she snatched her hand away.

What he was trying to achieve, she had no idea. He'd asked for someone to cook, and to clean his house. That's what she was doing. What she would continue to do.

He stared at her. Disappointment was written all over his face.

He opened his mouth to speak, but changed his mind and took a large gulp of his coffee instead.

The silence was deafening.

"Do you ever like to eat pie with supper?"

She watched as his face softened. "I do," he said, a grin forming. "Don't tell me you might mess it up," he said. "Because I know you won't."

He reached across the table and held her hand again. "I'm so glad you came, Amelia," he said.

She wasn't convinced it was *her* Samuel was glad about, more the food she made.

But she guessed that was a good start to their pending friendship.

Chapter Twelve

Samuel pushed the empty plate away from himself. "Another wonderful meal," he told his new bride. "I didn't expect anything like this," he said.

She leaned over and held his hand. Her response spread warmth all through his body.

Did that mean she was warming to him? She'd been so apprehensive when he'd done the same. But that was when she'd first arrived some days ago.

He'd never been a person to touch others, but it was different with Amelia. Whenever he was near her, he wanted to touch her, to hold her.

But they were near-strangers, and he was afraid to offend her sensibilities.

Going by the few gowns she had brought with her, she'd come from a well-to-do family.

He had no idea what had made her flee her family, but flee she had. They had to make the most of it.

She squeezed his hand, and that familiar zing ran up his arm. He put his free hand over hers.

"Thank you," she said quietly, then pulled her hand away to clear away the dishes.

"Don't go." His voice almost sounded as though he was begging her, and perhaps he was. Despite his best intentions, he was getting very used to having his wife around.

She smiled. "There's pie. Let me dish it up."

He nodded his acceptance, but it didn't reflect his thoughts. He would have sat there holding her hand all night if she'd let him.

"Apple pie," she said, putting a large slice in front of him. A bowl of cream followed it.

He grabbed her hand as she moved away. "Amelia," he said, a quiver in his voice. "Thank you."

She smiled down at him. How did he tell her she'd brightened up his life? That he now looked forward to each and every day.

He mentally shook himself. That was surely due to the wonderful meals she'd been presenting him with?

"You're welcome." She slid into her chair, and continued to stare at him.

"After supper, we'll retire to the sitting room." He wanted to get to know her. To find out more about her. Since she'd arrived, she'd revealed little about herself. She was still a virtual stranger, an outsider, despite the number of days they'd spent together. And that didn't sit well with Samuel.

"After I clean up," she said, but didn't look too happy about it.

Had she guessed what he had planned? It wasn't too big an ask, to learn about his new wife. Was it?

He stood and helped clear the table, but she glared at him. "Is something wrong?"

"It's my job to clear the table," she said, rounding on him. "That's what I'm here for, isn't it?"

His heart sank. Did she think she was here as a servant?

She was pushing herself to the limit, and now he knew why.

"Yes." The word was out before he could stop it. She stiffened and her lips pulled into a tight line. This was not going well, and was far from what he'd planned.

"No. That's not why you're here," he said, backtracking on his previous answer.

He retreated to the sitting room before he said something more to worsen the situation.

* * *

Samuel was leaning into the fireplace, stirring up the embers. Winter was setting in, but only a little snow had fallen.

She watched as his muscles worked their way across his back, and swallowed hard.

Amelia had never been interested in men. Those she'd been introduced to previously, the ones her father had wanted her to marry, were fools.

They were like silly little school boys who just wanted a play thing. And she was nobody's play thing.

She swallowed again. Her runaway thoughts reminded her of Uncle Cyrus and his shameful intentions.

"Ah, there you are," he said, and turned to stand up. The fire wasn't quite roaring yet, but she could feel the heat coming from it.

"The warmth is nice," she said, taking a step closer.

She rubbed her hands up her arms. It was more chilly than she'd realized. It was relatively warm in the kitchen with the wood stove burning all day.

He frowned. He stepped closer and ran his hands down her arms, something she was sure he wouldn't have done a week ago. "You're freezing. Go and put on a wrap."

He pulled her to him and enveloped her in a big hug. His warmth felt nice. Good. And she didn't want him to move.

And then he stepped back. The chill crept in once more.

Their eyes locked and she couldn't pull her gaze away.

Then she took stock of what she was doing, nodded and left the room. She returned wearing her thick overcoat.

He stared at her, his gaze questioning.

"It's all I have," she said softly, staring down at the floor. At that moment she felt totally ashamed. Having to admit such a thing made her feel humiliated.

Amelia had never wanted for anything in her life. Since her parent's deaths she'd been left in poverty, not possessing even the most basic of clothing.

She straightened her back, and flicked her chin up, just like her mother had taught her. "What did you want to discuss?"

He would never know the truth if she could help it.

By now the fire was roaring, and she moved closer to it. He joined her there, but she wished he'd go and sit down. Far away from her.

She felt things when he was close, and that would never do.

He reached across and took both her hands, holding them between his own.

"What happened? Why are you here, Amelia?" She could see the pity in his eyes, and that would never do.

She swallowed hard, then licked her lips. "Both my parents were killed in an accident," she said. "I was left with nothing. My uncle got everything."

It wasn't a lie. She hadn't said anything that wasn't true. She'd left out vital information, but she hadn't lied.

He let go of her hands and pulled her into him. "I'm sorry," he said gently into her ear.

She liked it when he held her like this. Amelia wasn't sure if it was his quiet strength, or simply the warmth he gave her. But she could get used to it very quickly.

She let herself sink into him, and rested her head on his shoulder. "What happened to all your clothes?"

She pulled back suddenly. Why did he have to keep asking questions? Especially questions she didn't want to answer.

He stared into her face. "You can tell me anything, Amelia," he said. "I'm your husband. No one will hear it from me."

"I don't want to talk about it." Her face hurt, she'd stiffened so much.

Then he did something she didn't expect. He leaned into her again and rubbed his hands over her back.

Why did he have to go and do that? It made her feel like she was important to him, and she knew that wasn't true.

She was just the housemaid.

"I'm sorry you've been through so much," he said, continuing to comfort her. "We'll organise clothes for you. And whatever else you need."

No one had ever been so kind to her. Not even her parents. To them it was all about appearances. It was never about her.

Amelia had been merely an accessory.

Without warning, tears slid down her face. She tried to pull away, but he held her tighter.

She stared into his face. He was so caring. After their rocky start, she was finally beginning to see the man beneath the rough exterior.

Chapter Thirteen

It was nearly three weeks since Amelia had arrived at the tiny township of Dayton Falls.

She'd gotten to know the people, had learned to cook, and had practically scrubbed the house from top to bottom.

But she and Samuel still hadn't consummated their marriage.

The subject hadn't come up, but she knew eventually it was something that would have to happen. Samuel was a man after all.

Tonight there was a dance at the church hall. Everyone had to take food to share.

As always, she was wrapped in Samuel's arms when she woke up. Safe and comfortable, the way she liked it.

Despite the problems they'd endured along the way, she felt they were beginning to feel like a real married couple.

She guessed that was a good thing.

She slowly slid toward the edge of the bed, and out of her husband's arms. She needed to make breakfast, and then prepare food for the dance tonight.

Nothing fancy, Samuel had told her. Something nice to share.

Her new gowns were hanging in the wardrobe, and she needed to decide what she would wear tonight, but right now, she had to go to the kitchen and get the wood stove warmed up.

"Where are you going," a sleepy voice asked.

She turned and stared into his face. She really could get used to seeing that face every morning. In fact she had gotten used to it.

He was a sweet man with a very handsome face. He reached out and grabbed her around the waist. "I miss you when you're not here," he said, trying to make her pity him.

She laughed. "I have to make breakfast, then something for the dance. Time to get up sleepyhead." She ruffled his jet black hair with her hands.

His eyes flew open, and he stared at her with intent, and grabbed her wrists.

Amelia swallowed. She knew that look, and quickly pulled out of his grip, then exited the bedroom, grabbing her robe as she went.

Samuel crept up behind her as she prepared breakfast. "Where did you go?"

His hands slid around her waist and he leaned in and kissed her neck gently.

He'd been the ultimate gentleman since she'd arrived. And she'd surely pushed him to the limit.

They'd slept in the same bed night after night, and he'd held her tight, but had never tried to do anything more.

She'd appreciated that.

But he was no longer a stranger.

He turned her in his arms and kissed her lips lightly, his eyes never leaving her face. A zing went through her.

She'd never been kissed by a man before, and she liked it.

"I'm falling in love with you, Mrs Thomas," he said, gazing into her eyes.

What did she say to his declaration of love? That she felt the same? That she'd never felt so loved, so cared for in her life?

"I have to finish making breakfast," she said instead, pushing him away. "Then I have to make something for the dance. What will everyone say say if we turn up with nothing?"

He pulled her closer and kissed her again. "I don't care," he whispered.

"Well I do. Besides," she said. "You have to go to work."

She pushed him aside again and finished what she was doing.

The kettle boiled and she made his coffee, placing it on the table.

"Drink your coffee," she said.

He cupped her face with his hands. "I have more important things to do," he said softly.

She stared into his eyes. His need was evident, but she wasn't ready.

"Breakfast is ready," she said forcefully. "Sit down and eat it."

He looked deflated, but complied. "You're a hard woman, Amelia Thomas," he said, and a grin crept across his face.

She laughed and sat opposite him.

"I'll finish work a little earlier today," he said. "To get ready for the dance."

He glanced up at her. She was nervous about going, and had told her husband.

He reached across the table and covered her hand with his own.

Warmth flooded her, and she didn't want him to remove it. Ever.

She stared down at their entwined hands. She wished he didn't have to work today, but knew he had a lot of orders to fill.

That was important, of course, but she longed for him to spend more time with her.

She sighed.

At least tonight at the dance they might have time together?

She sure hoped so.

The day progressed like any other day. She still had all her regular chores to do, meals to cook, but she also had to make something for the dance supper.

After flicking through the cookbook she decided to make a pound cake. It wasn't hard, but it would take a long time to cook.

She'd just finished cleaning up the mess from the cooking when she felt eyes burning into her back.

She quickly turned to see Samuel standing in the doorway, his eyes trained on her.

She straightened her skirts and touched the bun in her hair to ensure it was in place. She wanted to look nice for her husband.

"Luncheon will only be a moment. Sit down," she told him, then made his coffee and placed it on the table.

She had bacon and eggs cooking on the stove, but instead of sitting, he made his way purposely toward her.

She ignored him and pulled a plate out of the cupboard, ready for his food.

Her back to him, he came up behind her, and took the plate out of her hand.

She spun around. "I need that," she said, annoyed.

He held tight to it, and ignored her words.

"Amelia," he said, almost breathless. "I've waited so long for you."

He dropped the plate on the table and reached up and touched her hair, pulling out the clips.

He stared as her hair cascaded around her shoulders and down her back.

She reached up, but he grabbed her hands. "Leave it. I like it this way."

He ran his fingers through her hair, and Amelia stood mesmerized, not sure what to do next.

His face softened, his eyes transfixed on her lips. His fingers were suddenly touching her cheeks, caressing them.

Was he going to kiss her again? She had enjoyed his kiss this morning.

She stood watching him, her gaze on his face.

The sizzle of the frying pan alerted her to the fact the food was in jeopardy, and she snatched up the plate from the table.

She could see the disappointment on his face, and truth be told, she was equally disappointed.

"Sit," she told him again, and this time he did.

Chapter Fourteen

This was Amelia's first dance since she'd arrived, and she had no idea what to expect.

Samuel had told her everyone would be there. They came from far and wide, and it was the event no one was willing to miss.

She'd been to dances before, but not at Dayton Falls. Her parents had forced her to attend dozens of dances, all with the sole purpose of meeting a husband.

Those dances had been very high class. After all, what else would you expect in Westlake, Wyoming?

The part of town she'd lived in was made up of the crème de la crème – the high end of town. And monthly dances were all the rage.

Young women of high society attended every dance, and she was no different. But they were all in competition with each other, all vying for the richest men.

She felt like a piece of meat at the cattle sales, and hated every minute of it.

Samuel had explained this dance was nothing like those she'd attended in the past. They were casual and laid-back, and no one was going to judge her.

It was more a social event than anything. A time and place for the town's people to get together and get to know each other better.

Dayton Falls was big on community, and this was one of the ways they came together.

Many lived on the outskirts of town and rarely ventured in, except perhaps every few weeks to make their purchases at the Mercantile.

She'd been lucky. Once she'd settled into town Amelia had joined the women's auxiliary at the church. She thoroughly enjoyed it.

She was in the bedroom trying to choose a gown for the evening when Samuel strolled in. "Oh! You're early," she exclaimed, not prepared for his arrival.

"I said I'd be finishing early."

She had water on the stove for his bath, but didn't expect him quite so soon.

He leaned into her. "You smell divine. You've already had your bath." Disappointment flooded his voice.

They'd decided it would be appropriate to bathe tonight, so she'd taken the liberty while he was still at work.

She stared into his sad face. "I thought it would save time."

"I wanted to wash your back," he said, mischief written all over his face.

"Not in this lifetime," she muttered under her breath. "Oh, I'm sorry," she said out loud. "Maybe next time."

His face lit up, but she knew it would never happen – she wouldn't allow such a scandalous thing to occur!

She pushed past him and he stepped back. "I'll fill the bath for you." The water must nearly be ready.

As nervous as she was, she was looking forward to the evening's event. She hoped it would be everything Samuel had promised.

At least she knew those horrible catty women from Westlake wouldn't be there. That was a huge relief.

* * *

It was finally time to leave for the dance.

Samuel helped her into her warm overcoat. It was freezing outside, and there had even been a little snow.

Not a lot, but enough to know it had fallen. Amelia couldn't wait until there was thick snow covering the ground.

She pulled on her warm gloves, and they headed toward the church hall. It wasn't far, but in the cold, moist air, it felt like it was further.

Samuel reached for her hand, and his fingers entwined in hers. She felt safe with him, had almost from the start.

It was funny, he was a complete stranger when she'd arrived, but there was never any question that he might harm her.

And yet, with Uncle Cyrus that thought was always at the back of her mind – for as long as she could remember.

She shook the thought away. He would never find her, and she was safe right where she was.

They could hear the music coming from the dance even before they turned the corner. The place was lit up, and the sound was that of happiness.

Suddenly the music stopped and there was applause. Her heart filled with joy.

She began to almost run, and pulled Samuel along behind her.

"Steady down," he said. "The ground is slippery from the snow."

She nodded, but wasn't sure he could see her in the limited light.

As they entered the hall, she looked around, taking everything in. This was so different to those dances she'd attended in the past.

Everyone looked happy to be there, and were talking to others. Unlike the Westlake dances where everything was strained and all the young women were on display.

She swallowed hard. Amelia was so glad she no longer had to worry about all that nonsense.

"Amelia, Samuel!" Phoebe called to them from across the room. "I'm so pleased you both came."

She certainly seemed genuinely pleased.

Before she knew it, some of the ladies from the auxiliary surrounded her. Mrs Jensen took the sliced pound cake from her hands, and Mrs Green led her to the kitchen were some of the other women had congregated.

As she glanced back over her shoulder, Samuel was busy chatting to a few of the men. She didn't know them all, but she recognized Edward Horvard from the Mercantile, and Angus Doyle who was the town sheriff.

The music began again, and Amelia found herself tapping her foot in time with the beat. She desperately wanted to dance with her husband, but she was stuck in the kitchen, helping to prepare for the supper later on.

She needed to be patient.

As she glanced across the room, she saw Samuel staring in her direction. Was he missing her as much as she was missing him?

She shook the thought away. He looked as though he was enjoying himself. Goodness knows he worked long hours and didn't get much chance to spend his time with other men.

She needed to let him be.

"What do you think of our little dance?" It was Allie, the barber's wife. "This is your first one, am I right?"

Amelia turned to her. They'd only met a few times, but she really liked Allie. She was another mail order bride.

"Yes, it is, and I adore it. This is so much friendlier than any I've attended before."

Allie grinned. "Now all you have to do is dance with your handsome husband."

Allie moved forward and took her own husband by the hand. They were soon dancing to the beat of the music.

"Will you do me the honor?" Samuel stood in front of her, his hand outreached. He pulled Amelia onto the dance floor, and held her close.

As they shuffled around the floor, she leaned her head against his chest. His arms were around her waist, and he'd pulled her closer still.

She didn't complain. Amelia could have stayed there all night.

And then the music stopped.

She was reluctant to leave the comfort of her husband's arms, and stood right where she was. Soon the music began again.

This time the dance floor was crowded, and they could barely move. People were packed in and it became uncomfortable.

Samuel led her outside. They could still hear the music playing, but she could breathe. His arms went up around her again, and she looped hers around his waist.

She leaned her head against his chest, and gently swayed to the music.

It was better out here. Much more peaceful, more…intimate.

She looked up into her husband's face. He seemed more relaxed than he had for a very long time.

She was glad.

He worked far too hard, and deserved to have some relaxation time. Best of all, he was spending that time with her.

She groaned softly as she rested her head against him once more.

"What do you think of the dance," he asked, breaking the spell.

She looked up at him again. "I like it. It's fun."

He stared down at her, gazed at her lips. "It is," he said softly, then covered her lips with his own.

He took her by surprise, but she didn't mind. She was right where she wanted to be – standing close to her husband, him kissing her like she really mattered.

Chapter Fifteen

When they'd left home, Samuel wasn't certain he wanted to share Amelia with the rest of Dayton Falls.

Apart from attending church, they hadn't ventured out anywhere else. He enjoyed having her to himself.

But he could see she was having a ball, wandering around and talking to people she'd never met before.

She was a real social butterfly.

He didn't mind, so long as she always came back to him, and he knew she would.

It was hard to believe he'd fallen so hard for this petite woman. That he would even fall for someone so forthright and bossy.

He grinned against her silky hair.

That was just one of the things he loved about her. As much as he didn't want to admit it, he was in love with her.

They may not have been together long, but he couldn't bear to not have her around. It would shatter his heart into tiny pieces.

The music stopped again, but in his heart the music never stopped. Not while he had Amelia by his side.

It never would stop while his wife was in his heart.

He gazed down at her. "Amelia," he said softly, and she glanced up at him.

Her eyes sparkled in the moonlight. They looked like unshed tears, but she wasn't crying. The moon was reflecting her love.

"Samuel?" She seemed perplexed.

Her luscious lips opened, and to him that was an invitation. He leaned in and kissed her.

Gently at first, but then it became more urgent.

Her arms snaked up around his neck. He was never so glad to be outside in the cold air, away from prying eyes.

His hand slid down her back and gingerly touched her behind. His other hand slid to her breast.

She didn't protest.

Then he remembered where they were. At the church dance. Outside away from everyone else, granted, but still at church.

He pulled back, and his hands went to her back once more.

"I think we should leave," Amelia said quietly.

He nodded, but said nothing. He wasn't sure he could trust himself at that moment.

They collected their coats and headed for home. Not a word passed between them.

When they arrived back home, he turned to her. "We have unfinished business," he said.

She looked confused. "Unfinished business?"

"Like consummating our marriage."

He gently lifted her, and carried her into the bedroom. Amelia didn't protest.

* * *

She awoke in her husband's arms, and it felt wonderful.

Finally they were a real married couple. She wondered why they'd waited so long, but deep down knew the reason.

They didn't know each other at the start. They were complete strangers, and you didn't make love to total strangers, even if it was your legally married husband.

Becoming a mail order bride had been the hardest thing she'd ever done, but she wasn't sorry.

Especially now that the two of them had reconciled their love for each other.

She gently pulled out of his arms. It was Sunday and she needed to get organized. Needed to prepare something for the church luncheon.

She'd come to look forward to Sundays. It was one of the highlights of her week. Not only because she got to worship, but because of the people.

Dayton Falls had a lovely little community. People helped each other, and looked out for each other. That had never happened where she lived before.

It was everyone for themselves. It made her sad just thinking about it.

As she stood in front of the mirror putting her hair up, she was almost certain her husband would pull it down again, but not until he'd run his lips over her neck.

He was predictable like that.

It wouldn't be long and the cold would have truly set in. Winter was here already, and Christmas was on the way.

She couldn't wait to prepare for Christmas, and wondered what celebrations the church would organize.

She rolled out the pastry for a chicken pie, her contribution to today's luncheon, when she felt two strong arms snake around her waist.

"Good morning," he said, sleep still evident in his voice. It only took a moment, and his lips were on her neck.

He spun her around and began to pull the clips from her hair, preferring it to cascade down her back.

Of course she would put it back up before they left for church.

"Really, Samuel," she said. "I'm trying to make a pie for luncheon."

She tried to turn back, but he caught her before she could.

"Is it wrong to want to kiss my wife?"

He gazed into her eyes. It was evident he wanted to do more than kiss, but she was having none of it.

"Sit down," she said gently. "Your coffee will only be a moment."

He reluctantly did as he was told. "You're a tough woman, Mrs Thomas," he said. "But I love you for it." He grinned, and she found herself grinning too.

"I have to be, with the likes of yourself," she said, then chuckled.

"Chicken pie for luncheon sounds good," he said, rubbing his hands together.

Amelia could see herself spending the rest of her life with this handsome scoundrel.

Chapter Sixteen

Together they'd ventured into the forest and found a small tree to add to the sitting room.

Amelia decorated it with pinecones and paper chains, berries and dried flowers.

It looked so pretty.

She made a wreath out of pine branches, berries and holly leaves, and placed it in the middle of the table. It was a lovely centerpiece, and she'd enjoyed making it.

She figured it was time to start thinking about her Christmas menu.

The ladies auxiliary were putting together celebration baskets for those less fortunate than themselves. Amelia felt excited and privileged to be a part of it.

She'd made many new friends through the auxiliary, and the church, and it made her heart sing.

She pulled down a large porcelain bowl and began to throw ingredients into it.

She measured each ingredient and threw them into the bowl – raisins, currents, almonds. She chopped the mixed peel, and added the spices.

Her heart was filled with joy making these puddings with love for those who were not so blessed as themselves.

Samuel came up behind her and put his arms around her as he loved to do. "It's a wonderful thing you're doing, Amelia," he said with pride in his voice. "It will mean a lot to the receivers."

Her heart fluttered as it did whenever he was near.

"Oh!" She suddenly dropped the wooden spoon.

He turned her around. "What was that?" He looked genuinely concerned.

"I, I don't know," she said, feeling worried.

She put her hand to her stomach. "It's moving," she whispered.

Samuel gently put his hands to her stomach. He looked surprised as they moved around. Then grinned.

"I think we're going to have a little one," he said, continuing to grin.

"A baby? We're going to have a baby?" Her eyes welled with tears. "That's wonderful," she said, hugging her husband.

"It certainly is," he said against her silky hair, as he removed the offending clips.

Epilogue

One year later

As Amelia decorated the tree, little James crawled around the room, gathering up anything he could find.

Samuel stepped in and scooped him up.

"Mama," he called, as his father took control.

Samuel laughed. "Mama is busy. Papa is not so soft as Mama. You sit here and behave."

As much as he pretended otherwise, Samuel was just as lenient as she was.

Amelia stared out the window. "Look James," she said pointing. "It's snowing!"

The child jumped out of his father's arms and crawled to the window. "Snow." He didn't really understand what it was, but was fascinated by it.

Samuel stood behind him, then lifted the child so he could see better.

Amelia joined them. "Oh!" she squealed, then grinned.

"Samuel," she said. "How would you like another arrival?"

He put his hands to her stomach. "I think that would be wonderful," he said, then pulled her close. "I thank God for sending you to me. I love you so very much," he said, kissing her softly.

Amelia felt the same. She loved her little family, and loved the town of Dayton Falls.

From the Author

Thank you so much for reading my book – I hope you enjoyed it.

I would greatly appreciate you leaving a review where you purchased, even if it is only a one-liner. It helps to have my books more visible!

The next book in this series is *The Baker's Christmas Miracle*

About the Author

Multi-published, award-winning and bestselling author Cheryl Wright, former secretary, debt collector, account manager, writing coach, and shopping tour hostess, loves reading.

She writes both historical and contemporary western romance, as well as romantic suspense.

She lives in Melbourne, Australia, and is married with two adult children and has six grandchildren. When she's not writing, she can be found in her craft room making greeting cards.

Links

Website: *http://www.cheryl-wright.com/*

Facebook Reader Group:
https://www.facebook.com/groups/cherylwrightauthor/

Join My Newsletter:

https://cheryl-wright.com/newsletter/
(and receive a free book)